CLICK, CLACK, MOO
Cows That Type

by Doreen Cronin   pictures by Betsy Lewin

SIMON & SCHUSTER BOOKS FOR YOUNG READERS An imprint of Simon & Schuster Children's Publishing Division, 1230 Avenue of the Americas, New York, New York 10020. Text copyright © 2000 by Doreen Cronin. Illustrations copyright © 2000 by Betsy Lewin. All rights reserved including the right of reproduction in whole or in part in any form. SIMON & SCHUSTER BOOKS FOR YOUNG READERS is a trademark of Simon & Schuster. Book design by Anahid Hamparian. The text of this book is set in 30 point Filosofia Bold. 10 9 8 7 6 5 4 3 2 1 Library of Congress Cataloging-in-Publication Data: Cronin, Doreen. Click, clack, moo : cows that type / by Doreen Cronin ; pictures by Betsy Lewin. — Library bound ed. p. cm. Summary: When Farmer Brown's cows find a typewriter in the barn they start making demands, and go on strike when the farmer refuses to give them what they want. ISBN-13: 978-1-59961-088-7 ISBN-10: 1-59961-088-4 [1. Cows—Fiction. 2. Domestic animals—Fiction. 3. Typewriters—Fiction.] I. Lewin, Betsy, ill. II. Title. PZ7.C88135C1 2006 [E]—dc22 2006006014

CLICK, CLACK, MOO
Cows That Type

by Doreen Cronin   pictures by Betsy Lewin

Farmer Brown has a problem.
His cows like to type.
All day long he hears

Click, clack, **moo.**
   Click, clack, **moo.**
Clickety, clack, **moo.**

At first, he couldn't believe his ears.
Cows that type?

Click, clack, **moo.**
  Click, clack, **moo.**
Clickety, clack, **moo.**

Then, he couldn't believe his eyes.

Dear Farmer Brown,
The barn is very cold
at night.
We'd like some electric
blankets.

Sincerely,
The Cows

It was bad enough the cows had found the old typewriter in the barn, now they wanted electric blankets! "No way," said Farmer Brown. "No electric blankets."

So the cows went on strike. They left a note on the barn door.

Sorry.
We're closed.
No milk
today.

"No milk today!" cried Farmer Brown. In the background, he heard the cows busy at work:

Click, clack, **moo.**
Click, clack, **moo.**
Clickety, clack, **moo.**

The next day, he got another note:

Dear Farmer Brown,
The hens are cold too.
They'd like electric
blankets.
Sincerely,
The Cows

The cows were growing impatient with the farmer. They left a new note on the barn door.

"No eggs!" cried Farmer Brown.
In the background he heard
them.

Click, clack, **moo.**
  Click, clack, **moo.**
Clickety, clack, **moo.**

"Cows that type. Hens on strike! Whoever heard of such a thing? How can I run a farm with no milk and no eggs!" Farmer Brown was furious.

Farmer Brown got out his own typewriter.

Dear Cows and Hens:
There will be no electric blankets. You are cows and hens.
I demand milk and eggs.
Sincerely,
Farmer Brown

Duck was a neutral party, so he brought the ultimatum to the cows.

The cows held an emergency meeting. All the animals gathered around the barn to snoop, but none of them could understand Moo.

All night long, Farmer Brown waited for an answer.

Duck knocked on the door early the next morning. He handed Farmer Brown a note:

Dear Farmer Brown,
We will exchange our typewriter
for electric blankets.
Leave them outside the barn door
and we will send Duck over
with the typewriter.
Sincerely,
The Cows

Farmer Brown decided this was
a good deal. He left the blankets

next to the barn door and waited for Duck to come with the typewriter.

The next morning he got a note:

Dear Farmer Brown,
The pond is quite boring.
We'd like a diving board.
Sincerely,
The Ducks

Click, clack, **quack.**
Click, clack, **quack.**
Clickety, clack, **quack.**